THIS WALKER BOOK BELONGS TO:

_____

_____

_____

_____

For my darling Amy
A.D.

For Julie Chalmers
S.H.

First published 1995 by Walker Books Ltd
87 Vauxhall Walk, London SE11 5HJ

This edition published 2001

2 4 6 8 10 9 7 5 3 1

Text © 1995 Alan Durant
Illustrations © 1995 Sue Heap
Beta font © 2001 Cathy Gale

Printed in Hong Kong

British Library Cataloguing in Publication Data
A catalogue record for this book is
available from the British Library.

ISBN 0-7445-7579-6 (hb)
ISBN 0-7445-7835-3 (pb)

MOUSE PARTY

Alan Durant

illustrated by Sue Heap

WALKER BOOKS
AND SUBSIDIARIES
LONDON • BOSTON • SYDNEY

Mouse found a
deserted house and decided
to make his home there.
But it was a very big house
for such a small mouse and
he felt a little lonely.

"I know," he thought,
"I'll have a party." So he sent
invitations to all his friends.

The first to arrive were...

Cat with a mat

and **Dog** with a **log**.

Then came **Hare** with a **chair**,

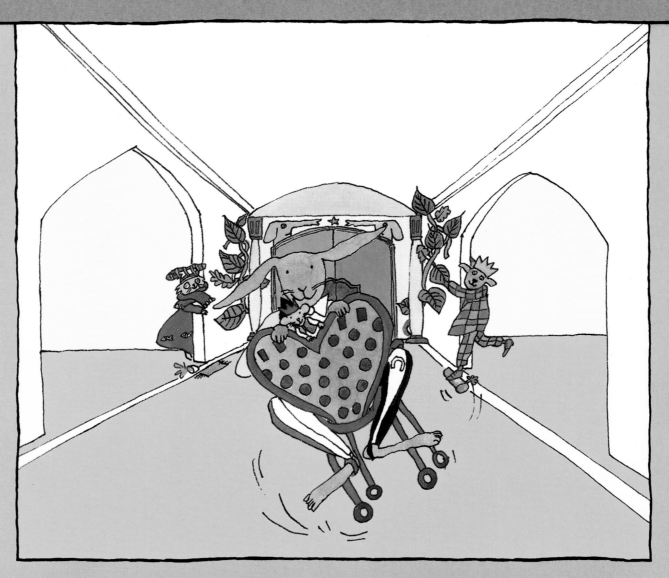

Owl with a **towel**,

Giraffe with a bath,

Hen with a **pen**,

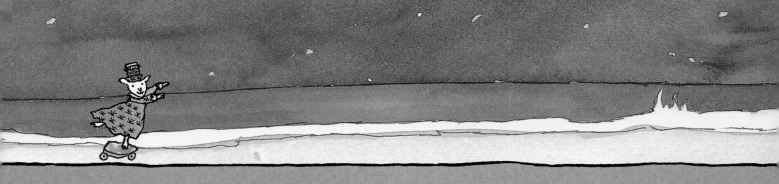

Lamb with some jam,

Rat with a bat in a hat,

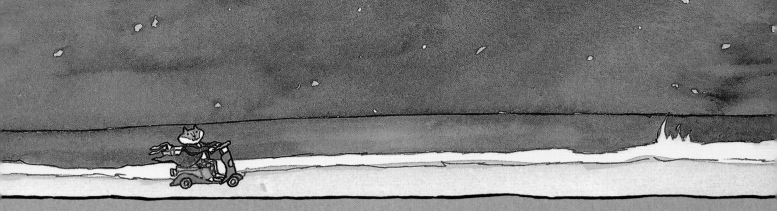

and **Fox** with a **box** full of **lots** and **lots**

of different kinds and colours of **socks**.

"Let's party!" said Mouse.   But...

Rat-a-

tat-tat!

It was an elephant with two trunks.
He was blowing through one
and carrying the other.
"Hello," said Mouse.
"Welcome to my house."

"*Your* house?" said the elephant and he looked rather cross. "I've just been away on a long holiday. This house, I must tell you, is mine!"

"Oh," said Cat, Lamb, Hare, Rat and Bat.

"Oh," said Hen, Dog, Owl,
Fox and Giraffe.

But, "Come in, come in!" said Mouse. "You're just in time for the party."

"A party ... for me?" said Elephant.
"Oh my! Yippee!"

So they drank and they ate
and they danced until late

and had the most marvellous party.

And later, when the
guests had all gone home,
leaving Elephant and
Mouse alone, Elephant said,
"I think, little Mouse, perhaps
it's true, there's room for
us both in this house,
don't you?"

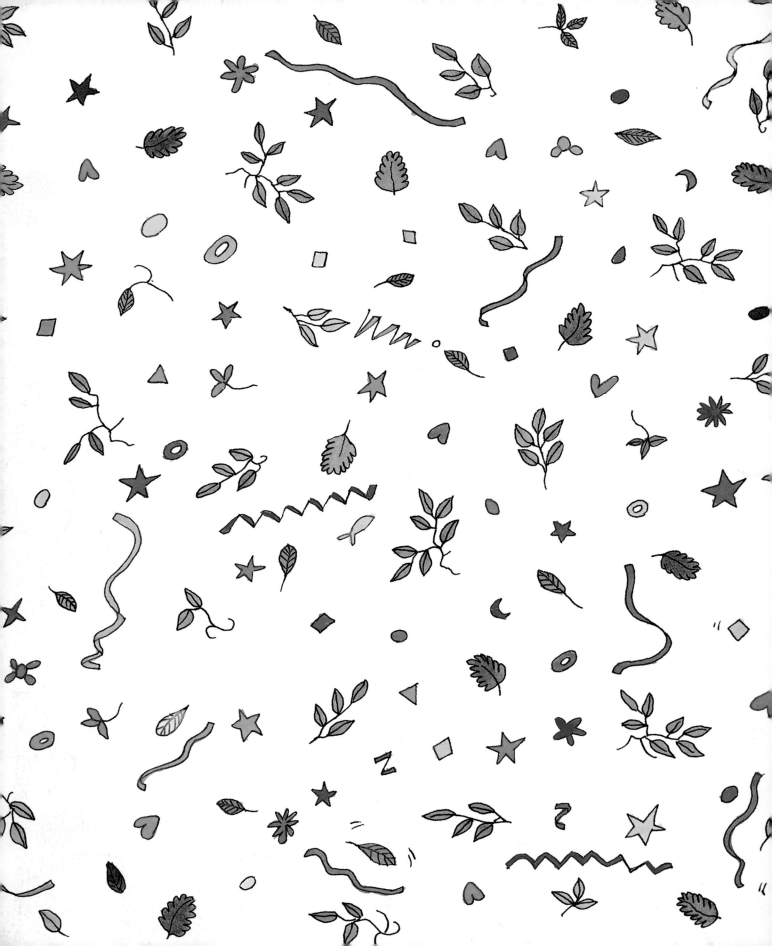

ALAN DURANT says **Mouse Party** began with the rhyme *mouse in a house*. "Then I started to think of other rhymes. At one time there was a cow with a plough, but she got cut on about the tenth redraft. Some of the rhymes aren't proper rhymes at all – giraffe with a bath, owl with a towel – but the sounds are similar and that's good enough for me! Can you think of animal guests of your own and the rhyming things they might bring? Take a good look at the pictures, because they tell stories that aren't in the words. Study the hen, for example, and her amazing hatching-egg dress, see what happens to the fish on the cat's dress – and don't miss the extraordinary dancing socks!"

Alan has written many stories for children of all ages. He lives with his wife, three children and an aged deaf cat (without a mat) in Surrey.

SUE HEAP enjoyed creating the details for the animals in this story. "You can tell a lot about their personalities by what they wear and what they drive. The hen's dress happened purely in the spirit of partying and mischief on my part!" Sue is also the illustrator of the Smarties Book Prize Winner *Cowboy Baby* (which she wrote), as well as *Cowboy Kid*, *Little Chicken Chicken* and *Night-night, Knight*. She lives in Oxfordshire.

ISBN 0-7445-5236-2 (pb)

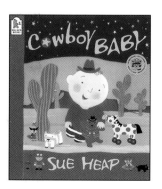

ISBN 0-7445-6330-5 (pb)

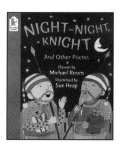

ISBN 0-7445-6999-0 (pb)